Library of Congress Control Number: 2021900761

ISBN 978-1-7365048-0-2 (Hardback)

ISBN 978-1-7365048-1-9 (Paperback)

Published by: LaRue Ramey

Distributed by: OADPublications

A portion of OAD Publications proceeds go to the

Once A Dream Foundation - a nonprofit organization.

To learn more about the author and OAD Publications visit:

www.OADPublications.com

Social Media: @OADPublications

To learn more about the Once A Dream Foundation visit:

www.OnceADream.org

Social Media: @OnceADreamFoundation

This book is dedicated to every boy and girl that face what only

appears to be impossible.

You can do ALL things through Christ who gives you strength.

(Philippians 4:13)

Aden, Sunny & Dominic (DK) 🖤

Everyone will be Amazed!

Written by LaRue Ramey

Illustrated by Dilmi Amarasinghe

I'm going to be an Olympian!

I'm going to win the Olympic gold in swimming, and then I'm going to be a figure skater.

I am going to run one hundred miles
straight without even stopping,
and then I am going to paint a masterpiece
with my toes.

It will be better than Picasso's.

I'm going to tap dance all the way across the
Chesapeake Bay Bridge,
and then I'm going to jump over
five monster trucks.

Everyone will be amazed!

I'm going to join the circus and become the most graceful trapeze artist the world has ever seen. People will travel from all over just to see me fly!

" Encore, Encore,"
they'll scream as I proudly walk through
rose petals thrown at my feet.

I'm going to win first place in the Tour de France.

The headlines will read,
"Girl Takes First Place with Unbeatable Record,"
and everyone will be amazed!

• Monday, June 7, Issue

NEWS FOR TODAY

WORLD NEWS

TOUR DE FRANCE : FINISH OF THE FINAL STAGE

"Girl Takes First Place with Unbeatable Record "

American female cyclist has become the youngest rider and the first woman in history to win the Tour de France. Crossing the finish line in Paris for eventual race victory, following her stunning uphill time trial on Stage 20, sees she become the first-youngest overall champion in race history. In total, she cycled over 2,200 miles (3,500 kilometers) from Brest, Brittany, to Paris, in the Celtic region of Brittany, France. It took her 21 days, 2 hours, and 48 minutes.

"I'm the happiest girl in the world. I just won the Tour de France!," she

I'm going to become a firefighter and rescue people from burning buildings.

I'll climb the highest redwood tree
to save a cat who can't
get down on its own.
My bravery will be nonpareil.

I'm going to China just so I can walk 128 floors
to the very top of the
Shanghai Tower.

When I get back to North America, I'm going to walk a tightrope across Niagara Falls.
The sounds of people cheering will echo off the surrounding rocks, and everyone will be amazed!

I'm going to become a ballerina
and star in famous Ballets
all over the nations.

My pliés and pirouettes will be done with
so much poise and elegance
that I will receive standing ovations
after every sold-out show.

I'm going to swim with a pod of dolphins
in Bahamian waters.

They'll clap their fins together, because even
they will be impressed
with how skilled I am
at jumping in and out of the ocean!

I'm going to hike through
the Amazon rainforest wearing
sunflower printed waterproof boots,
and several pairs of socks,
so my toes will stay dry.

I'll make friends with
toucans, blue butterflies, scarlet macaws,
anteaters, two-toed sloths,
and even poisonous dart frogs! I won't go near
those though. They can be admired from afar!

On my shoulder will sit a spider monkey
that I'll name Pete.
When I feed Pete bananas and aerial roots,
he'll dance and clap his little hands.

When I start to dance with him
everyone will be amazed.

Look at me going on, and on!
I have so much to do!
I'd better get started.
This is going to be
so exciting -
everyone will be so amazed!

"But you don't even have legs!"

And YOU don't even have dreams!

Do you know what?
She did it.
And, Everyone Was Amazed.

CPSIA information can be obtained
at www.ICGtesting.com
Printed in the USA
LVHW070744180621
690564LV00018B/1401